AND ME, COYOTE!

By Betty Baker
Pictures by Maria Horvath

MACMILLAN PUBLISHING CO., INC., New York

COLLIER MACMILLAN PUBLISHERS, London

Macmillan Publishing Co., Inc.
866 Third Avenue, New York, N.Y. 10022
Collier Macmillan Canada, Inc.
Printed in the United States of America

10 9 8 7 6 5 4 3 2 1

Library of Congress Cataloging in Publication Data
Baker, Betty.   And me, coyote!
Summary: The author retells material from Native
American creation legends in which World Maker, Blind
Man, and Coyote shape the world and its inhabitants.
[1. Creation—Fiction]
I. Horvath, Maria, date. ill.   II. Title.
PZ7.B1693Am 1982 [E] 82-7134
ISBN 0-02-708280-6 AACR2

ong ago, before the world was made, water was everywhere. But deep in the water were Coyote, World Maker and World Maker's brother.

Coyote could not see World Maker and his brother. He had to keep his eyes tight shut. But Coyote knew they were there. And he knew when they started to move.

He tried to call, "Wait for me!" But bitter water ran into his mouth. He choked and coughed so he could not swim. When World Maker's brother swam by, Coyote grabbed a leg and held on.

World Maker's brother yelled and kicked his leg, but Coyote held tight. He held on until they reached the top of the water.

Coyote and World Maker kept their eyes shut all the way to the top. But when the brother yelled, he opened his eyes. When his head came out of the water, he was blind.

"Don't worry," Coyote told him. "I'll tell you everything."

"Well, then," said Blind Man, "tell me! What do you see?"

"Water," said Coyote.

"Isn't there some place that isn't water?" said Blind Man.

"Not yet," World Maker said. Then he said, "Sneeze, Coyote!"

And Coyote did. He sneezed little red ants.

"Sneeze again," World Maker told him.

Coyote sneezed again and again. He sneezed until his sides hurt and little red ants covered the water. Then World Maker began to sing. He sang the ants into land.

"What is he doing?" said Blind Man.

"We are making land," Coyote told him. "World Maker and me, Coyote!"

Coyote climbed onto the land and helped pull Blind Man out of the water.

"This is better," Coyote said. Then he sniffed and said, "Isn't there anything to eat?"

World Maker laughed.

"Shake, Coyote," he said.

Coyote shook himself. Drops of water flew everywhere. Blind Man yelled, but World Maker began to sing. He sang the drops into corn and beans, melons and berries, flowers and grasses and trees.

Coyote ate a melon.

"This is good," he said and ate another.

"What are you doing?" said Blind Man.

"We are making things grow," Coyote told him. "World Maker and me."

"I can do that, too," said Blind Man.

And he did. But his plants had stickers. So did the fruit.

"I can't eat those," Coyote told him.

"I don't want you to," said Blind Man.

World Maker took mud and began to shape animals.

"More mice and rabbits," Coyote told him. "And not too many wolves and bears."

"What is he doing?" said Blind Man.

Coyote told him.

"I can shape animals, too," said Blind Man.

And he did. But his animals had webbed feet and flat noses and tails. Coyote laughed at them and made Blind Man angry.

"They do look strange," World Maker said. "Maybe they can live in the water."

He pushed his brother's animals into the water. That made Blind Man even angrier.

"You'll be sorry," he told his brother. "You, too," he told Coyote.

Blind Man jumped in the water but he did not swim away. He began to sink. And as he sank, the water around him began to turn. Faster and faster it turned and all kinds of sickness came spinning up.

World Maker put his foot on the spinning water.

Coyote sneezed but he didn't sneeze ants.

"My nose is hot and runny," he said. "And my neck hurts. What is the matter?"

"You are sick," World Maker told him. "My foot didn't cover all of the whirlpool. Some sickness got out."

"That's because it's so dark," said Coyote. "I can't see to hunt, either."

World Maker smiled. "All right, Coyote, I'll make you some light."

He licked his finger and dabbed at the sky. Where he dabbed, light showed. He dabbed all over, making stars.

"Very pretty," Coyote said, "but they don't make enough light for hunting."

"If you can see other animals," World Maker told him, "they can see you, too."

But Coyote didn't care. He was sick and his nose was stuffed.

"I have to see to hunt," he said. "I can't smell now."

World Maker licked his finger again. He rubbed a circle on the sky and made the moon. To cheer Coyote, he drew a rabbit on it. Coyote tried to call to the rabbit, but his throat hurt too much.

"I feel terrible," he said. "I'm sick and very cold. If only I could get warm."

"Poor Coyote," World Maker said. He licked his finger and made the sun.

"This is better," said Coyote, and he stretched out in the sunshine and went to sleep.

World Maker began to sing. And as he sang, he made a spear. When he drew a line with his spear, dirt piled up along the sides and water flowed into it. All around the world he went, dragging his spear, making rivers and mountains.

When Coyote woke, he could smell again and his neck didn't hurt. Far away, World Maker was singing.

"I better go see what he's making now," Coyote said.

And he did. But he stopped to sniff and dig here and there. Dirt flew and some fell in the rivers and blocked them. Some parts of the rivers flooded; others went dry.

"I like that," said Coyote, and he blocked some rivers on purpose. He was so busy he never caught up with World Maker.

When he came back to where he'd started, the animals said, "Where have you been, Coyote?"

"I've been making the world," Coyote told them.

The animals laughed. "World Maker made the world," they said. "We saw him."

"But I helped," Coyote said.

The animals went to World Maker and said, "Coyote says he helped make the world. Did he?"

World Maker smiled and said, "The world would not be the same without him."

"There," said Coyote, "that means I helped."

"We want to help, too," the animals said.

"You're too late," Coyote told them. "The world is all made."

"Not quite," World Maker said. "There is one more thing to make."

"What?" they wanted to know.

"People," World Maker told them.

"We want to help," the animals said.

"You don't know how," said Coyote. "You don't even know how people should look."

"We do! We do!" the animals said.

"Good," World Maker said. "Then you may make people. Coyote will help you."

"Yes," said Coyote. "You must shape people out of mud."

Mud was hard to shape. Most of the animals could only make a lump, but Lizard's hands were small and neat. The shape he made was very like him.

Coyote said, "We'll tell Lizard how people should look and he will shape one."

The animals agreed.

"He must have four legs," they said.

Lizard made a shape with four legs.

"He should stand on his back legs like me," said Bear.

"Then he'll need a long tail to lean on," said Mouse.

Lizard changed the shape. He made it big and fat, standing on its back legs and a long thin tail.

"He needs a bigger jaw," said Wolf, "so his teeth can be long and strong."

"He needs horns to fight with," said Deer.

"And long ears to hear well," said Rabbit.

"And wings," said Jay. "He has to have wings."

"And his eyes must be big and round," said Owl. "How else will he see at night?"

Lizard ran up and down, adding all the things the animals wanted.

"That looks terrible!" said Coyote.

The animals walked around the shape. They looked at it this way and that.

"You are right," they told Coyote. "It is terrible."

"He'll never fly with those horns," said Jay.

"He needs horns to fight," said Deer.

"He can't fight with those silly ears," said Wolf. "They'll get bitten off."

"Those ears are not silly!" said Rabbit. "It's the tail that's silly."

"It is not!" said Mouse.

The animals ran around the shape, pulling things off and putting things back, yelling and pushing and kicking.

Lizard dug a hole and hid in it.

Coyote went to find World Maker. World Maker was making a shape out of red mud. Coyote sat down beside him.

"Those animals can't make people," Coyote told him. "They think people should look just like them."

"How should they look?" World Maker said. And he set the shape in the sun to dry.

"The way you make them," Coyote said. "But if people don't have wings or horns or big ears or wolf teeth, they'd better be smart like me."

World Maker smiled.

"Are you going to make them smart?" said Coyote.

"Yes," said World Maker.

Coyote waited, then he said, "When?"

"When they are dry," World Maker told him. Then he took more mud and began to shape another person.

"How many people are you going to make?" said Coyote.

"Two of each color of earth," World Maker said.

"That's going to take a long time," said Coyote, and he went to find something to eat.

When he came back, World Maker was gone. But standing in the sun were people, two of each color of earth.

"If they are dry," Coyote said, "I can tell World Maker and he can make them smart."

Coyote poked a brown one with his nose. The person was still soft. Coyote's nose made a dent in the belly.

"Maybe the pink ones are dry," said Coyote.

They were still soft, too. Coyote poked them all, the red and the black, the yellow and white and the colors in between. Not one of them was dry and Coyote's nose left a dent in each belly. When World Maker saw them, he laughed.

"Coyote has been helping again," he said.

But Coyote had gone to help the animals. Only Lizard was there, sunning himself on a big pile of mud.

"Where are the others?" Coyote said.

"Gone." Lizard waved a claw. "In different directions and very angry."

"Where is the person they made?" said Coyote.

"Here." Lizard nodded at the pile of mud. "They said nobody can make people."

"We did," said Coyote. "World Maker and me."

"Do they have horns and strong teeth?" said Lizard. "Or wings and big eyes and long ears?"

"No," said Coyote. "People don't need any of those. They're going to be smart like me."

Then they heard World Maker singing.

"Come!" Coyote told Lizard. "Come see the wonderful people we made, World Maker and me, Coyote!"